My Home
Bay

Anne Laurel Carter
Illustrated by Alan and Lea Daniel

Red Deer Press

"*P*lease get out of the car, Gwyn," Mom begs.

The new house looks asleep, eyes shuttered, behind a mess of uncombed trees. Mom made us leave Vancouver. She wants to live here, in Mahone Bay, near her brother.

Dad glares at me. "You've sulked from west coast to east, across the second largest country in the world. I think that's far enough."

Linden points beyond the trees. "What's that?"

"Our salt marsh," Mom says. "The water's high. Tide must be in."

"Please, Gwynie! Let's go play."

Linden's too little to care about moving. I only agreed because Mom and Dad made three promises. I wish I'd said no.

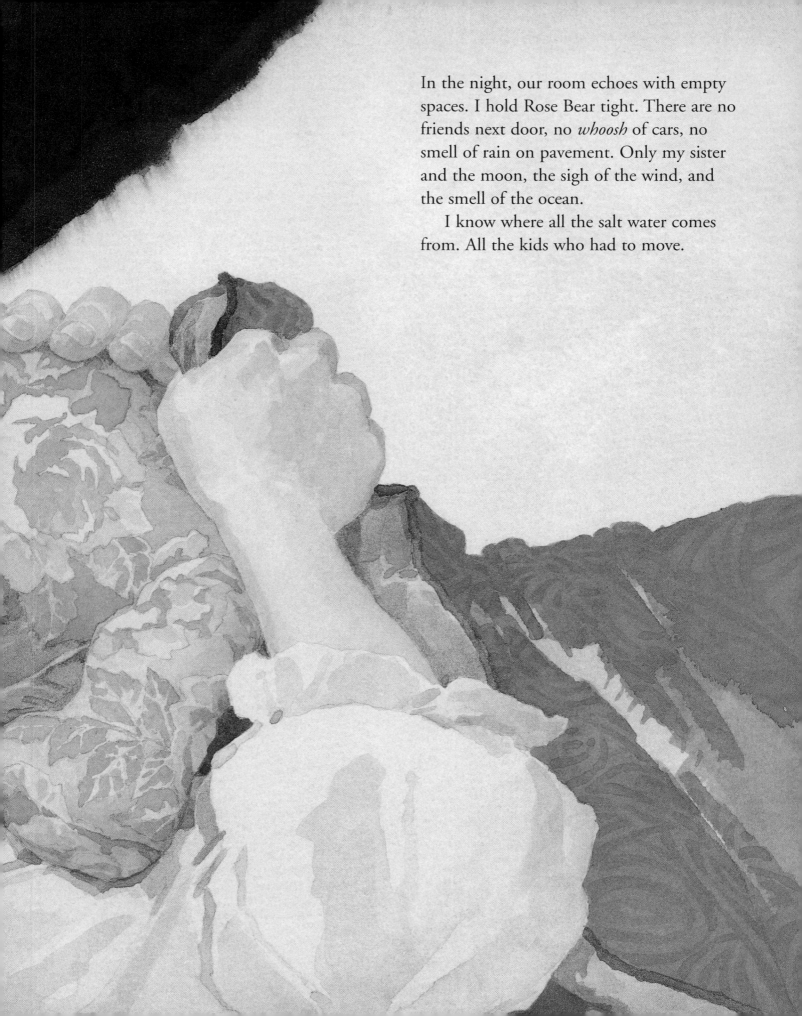

In the night, our room echoes with empty spaces. I hold Rose Bear tight. There are no friends next door, no *whoosh* of cars, no smell of rain on pavement. Only my sister and the moon, the sigh of the wind, and the smell of the ocean.

I know where all the salt water comes from. All the kids who had to move.

Linden wakes up.

"Don't cry." She hugs me. "Remember the promises? You're going to play with Fiddle." Her eyes grow big in the moonlight. "Gwynie, who's Fiddle? A cat?"

I sniff. "A fiddle's a musical instrument, like Dad's accordion. They promised I'd learn to play one here."

All summer Mom and Dad clear out overgrown hackmatack. They paint the house the same color as the driftwood on the beach. Linden and I plant irises and lupins in pockets of rocks.

I ask about the three promises. "Soon," Mom tells me.

For my birthday, I get a half-sized fiddle.

I pull the bow across one string. *Erreee.* Linden covers her ears.

On the first day of school, Linden
runs after me. She stuffs the fiddle
in my schoolbag.

"Ask your teacher for help," she whispers.

On the school bus, Megan from down the road lets me sit with her.

Soon she points to the bell tower on the town's old schoolhouse, so different from my brand-new school in Vancouver.

"The bell used to ring," Megan says. "But a ghost stole the clapper."

Inside, the school smells of wood. The floors creak. The stairs dip in the middle, worn down by a hundred years of feet. I won't let *my* feet walk there. I hold the banister and tiptoe up the side.

After school, I show Megan our salt marsh.
We find cranberries hidden under shiny
dark leaves, red and white ones that make
our mouths pucker.

It's low tide and there are little puddles
of water between big islands of grass.

"There's a sweet marsh up the road,"
Megan says. "We'll skate there in the
winter. The tides won't wreck the ice."

We climb into my favorite pine tree,
and I tell Megan about the second promise.
"They promised us a tree house."

Linden nods. "Gwynie will see right
back to Vancouver whenever she wants."

I roll my eyes. "No tree is high enough
for that."

On weekends, Uncle Peter takes us out on his boat. "Look over there," he says. "That's my farm."

"You grow water?" asks Linden.

Uncle Peter laughs. "My crops are below." He stops beside a row of white buoys, bobbing on the waves, and pulls up a netted sock crammed with shells. "Mussels," he says. "They grow in the ocean."

Linden shakes her head. "Silly Uncle Peter. Muscles grow on your arm."

Aunt Barbara comes for dinner, and Tom, the artist who lives on the point. Mom steams the mussels. The adults suck them from the shell. *Yuck!*

Dad makes cranberry pancakes, and we smother them with maple syrup from the neighbor's sugar bush.

Linden says, "Farms in the ocean. Syrup in a bush. Everything's mixed up out here."

Everybody laughs. Poor Linden. I don't feel mixed up anymore. Outside, the hackmatacks are a cheerful yellow, remembering summer.

In November, the birches are bare. Mom and Dad build the tree house in my favorite pine. The branches spiral up like a staircase.

Linden and I play top-of-the-world.

"Can you see Vancouver?" Linden asks. Her hands telescope over her eyes.

"No, but look that way." I point to Mahone Bay. "You can see Uncle Peter's farm."

It's high tide. Big lakes of water surround little islands in the salt marsh. A kingfisher dives for fish and disappears. Ship clouds sail across the blue sky. "I guess everything moves," I say.

"Not us," Linden says. "Never again."

I giggle. "Mom and Dad are stuck on the third promise."

"You shouldn't have asked for a horse," Linden grumbles. "We don't have a barn. We have a salt marsh."

"I wanted something hard. As hard as moving was for me."

"We could've had a real pet by now. I want a hamster or a cat for Christmas."

Linden's right. But I can't give in. "I asked for a pet that lives in the country."

"Silly Gwyn." Linden pouts. *"Cats* live in the country."

The afternoon before Christmas, Linden
and I climb the branch staircase to the top
of the world. Below us the salt marsh seems
wrapped in white tissue paper.

The fog rushes in and suddenly we're
alone. I turn around. The windows of our
house wink, calling us back.

"We better get home before we get lost,"
I say, holding Linden's hand.

Dad's written a song about Mahone Bay. Only Linden sings, "My home bay."

"What's that racket?" calls Uncle Peter.

"It's not a racket," Linden says. "It's Dad's new song."

There's a big gift on the bookcase beside the tree.

"It's something special. You can open it now," Mom says hopefully.

I know it holds the third promise. I should have backed down. What if it's a toy horse? I'm too big for a toy horse. I'm afraid to look.

Not Linden. She runs right over and rips off the paper.

It's an aquarium full of . . .

. . . "Seahorses," I whisper, kneeling beside Linden, our faces against the glass.

"Oh, Gwynie," Linden says. Her eyes are round with wonder. "It's better than a cat."

All afternoon we watch the tiny seahorses dance on their curly-swirly tails.

Outside, ribbons of white fog loop past our windows, then twirl away, carried by a breeze off my home bay.

Northern Lights Books for Children are published by
Red Deer Press
813 MacKimmie Library Tower
2500 University Drive N.W.
Calgary Alberta Canada T2N 1N4
www.reddeerpress.com

Credits
Edited for the Press by Peter Carver
Cover and text design by Blair Kerrigan/Glyphics
Printed and bound in Canada by Friesens for Red Deer Press

Acknowledgments
Financial support provided by the Canada Council, the Department of Canadian Heritage, the Alberta Foundation for the Arts, a beneficiary of the Lottery Fund of the Government of Alberta, and the University of Calgary.

COMMITTED TO THE DEVELOPMENT OF CULTURE AND THE ARTS

Canada

THE CANADA COUNCIL | LE CONSEIL DES ARTS
FOR THE ARTS | DU CANADA
SINCE 1957 | DEPUIS 1957

National Library of Canada Cataloguing in Publication Data
Carter, Anne, 1953-
My home bay / Anne Laurel Carter ; illustrator, Alan Daniel, Lea Daniel.
(Northern lights books for children)
ISBN 0-88995-284-1
I. Daniel, Alan, 1939- II. Daniel, Lea. III. Title. IV. Series.
PS8555.A7727M93 2003   jC813'.54   C2003-910214-9
PZ7.C2427My 2003

5 4 3 2 1

For Gwyneth
– Anne Laurel Carter

For Gwyn, Linden, Laurel and Reid
– Alan & Lea Daniel